Charles Schulz

by Julie Murray

Abdo
CHILDREN'S AUTHORS
Kids

Abdo Kids Jumbo is an Imprint of Abdo Kids
abdobooks.com

abdobooks.com

Published by Abdo Kids, a division of ABDO, P.O. Box 398166, Minneapolis, Minnesota 55439. Copyright © 2022 by Abdo Consulting Group, Inc. International copyrights reserved in all countries. No part of this book may be reproduced in any form without written permission from the publisher. Abdo Kids Jumbo™ is a trademark and logo of Abdo Kids.

Printed in the United States of America, North Mankato, Minnesota.

102021

012022

 THIS BOOK CONTAINS RECYCLED MATERIALS

Photo Credits: Alamy, Getty Images, iStock, newscom, Seth Poppel/Yearbook Library, Shutterstock PREMIER, p13,15: PEANUTS © Peanuts Worldwide LLC. Dist. By ANDREWS MCMEEL SYNDICATION. Reprinted with permission. All rights reserved.

Production Contributors: Teddy Borth, Jennie Forsberg, Grace Hansen
Design Contributors: Candice Keimig, Pakou Moua

Library of Congress Control Number: 2020948015

Publisher's Cataloging-in-Publication Data

Names: Murray, Julie, author.

Title: Charles Schulz / by Julie Murray

Description: Minneapolis, Minnesota : Abdo Kids, 2022 | Series: Children's authors | Includes online resources and index.

Identifiers: ISBN 9781098207205 (lib. bdg.) | ISBN 9781098208042 (ebook) | ISBN 9781098208462 (Read-to-Me ebook)

Subjects: LCSH: Schulz, Charles M. (Charles Monroe), 1922-2000--Juvenile literature. | Authors--Biography--Juvenile literature. | Children's books--Juvenile literature.

Classification: DDC 809.8928--dc23

Table of Contents

Early Years

Charles Monroe Schulz was born on November 26, 1922, in Minneapolis, Minnesota. He grew up in the nearby capital city of St. Paul.

Minneapolis, Minnesota

Charles loved drawing comic book characters from a young age. He learned more about drawing and **cartooning** in high school.

In 1947, Schulz began creating a weekly, single-panel comic strip for the *St. Paul Pioneer Press*. It was called *Li'l Folks*.

9

Peanuts

In 1950, Schulz got his cartoon strip **syndicated**. Schulz was asked to retitle *Li'l Folks*. It would be known as *Peanuts*.

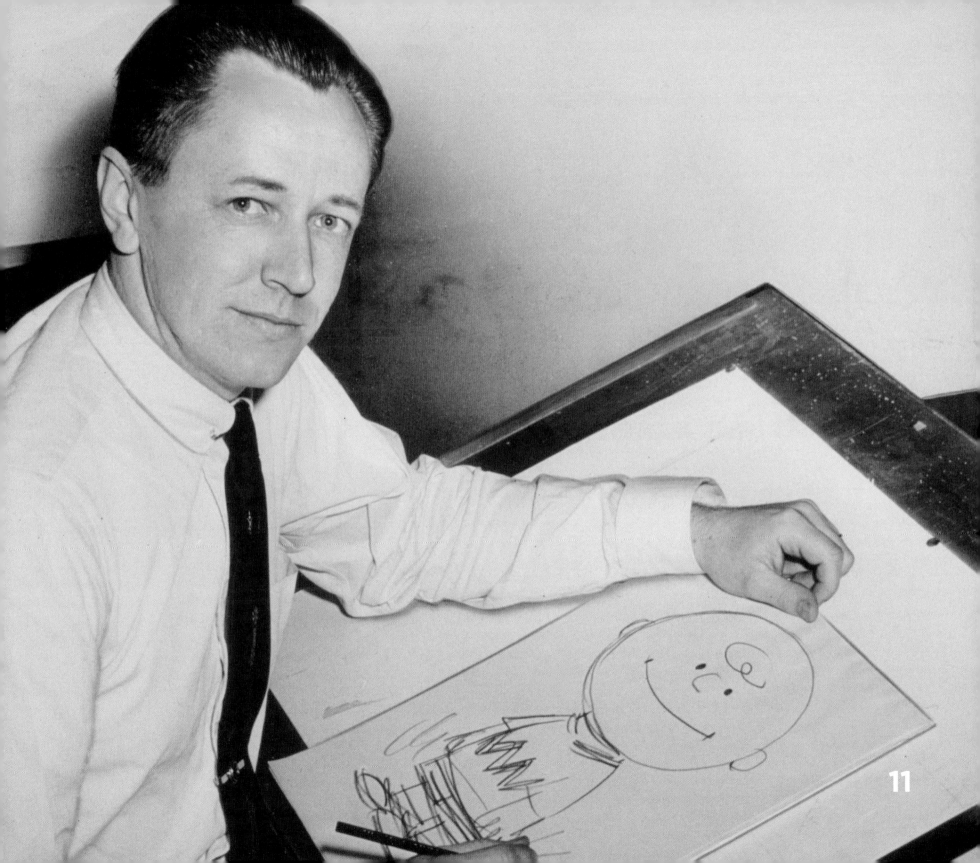

Peanuts first ran on October 2, 1950 in seven newspapers. It had four panels and featured four characters. They were Charlie Brown, Snoopy, Patty, and Shermy.

Peanuts • October 21, 1950

13

Interest in *Peanuts* grew. Many newspapers wanted to run the comic strip. Schulz continued to add characters over the years. Lucy, Linus, and Schroeder became well-loved too.

Peanuts • **March 15, 1953**

Schulz used his childhood memories as **inspiration** for Charlie Brown and the *Peanuts* gang. People loved the little kid characters with grown-up thoughts.

PSYCHIATRIC HELP 5¢

THE DOCTOR IS IN

Schulz helped create many *Peanuts* books, TV shows, and movies over the years. *A Charlie Brown Christmas* was a very popular TV special. It **debuted** in 1965.

Death & Legacy

Charles Schulz died on February 12, 2000. He entertained people with his characters for more than 50 years. People still enjoy *Peanuts* today!

Timeline

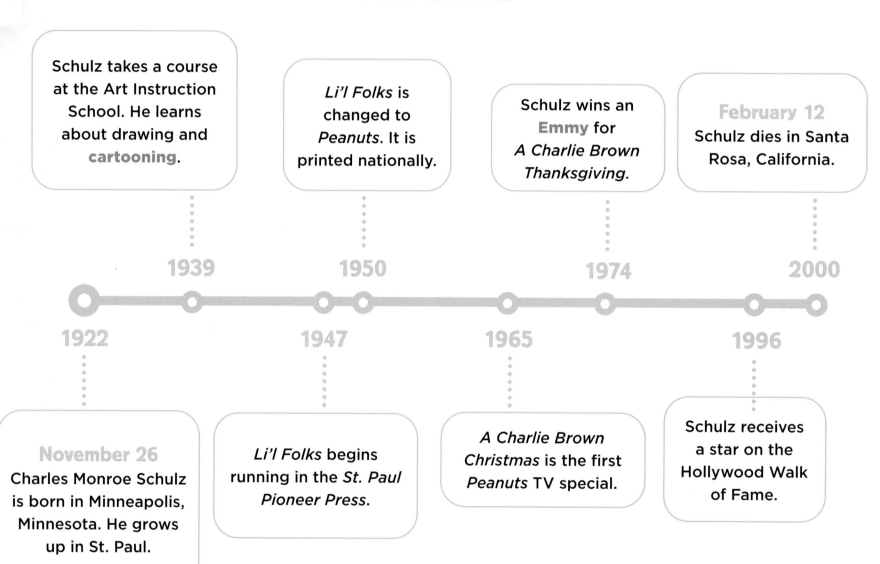

Schulz takes a course at the Art Instruction School. He learns about drawing and **cartooning**.

Li'l Folks is changed to *Peanuts*. It is printed nationally.

Schulz wins an **Emmy** for *A Charlie Brown Thanksgiving.*

February 12
Schulz dies in Santa Rosa, California.

1939

1950

1974

2000

1922

1947

1965

1996

November 26
Charles Monroe Schulz is born in Minneapolis, Minnesota. He grows up in St. Paul.

Li'l Folks begins running in the *St. Paul Pioneer Press*.

A Charlie Brown Christmas is the first *Peanuts* TV special.

Schulz receives a star on the Hollywood Walk of Fame.

22

Glossary

cartooning – the activity or occupation of drawing cartoons for newspapers or magazines.

debuted – presented to an audience for the first time.

Emmy – an award given annually to an outstanding television program or performer.

inspiration – someone or something that gives a person ideas for doing something.

syndicated – sold to several different newspapers, magazines, television programs, etc.

Index

Abdo Kids
ONLINE
FREE! ONLINE MULTIMEDIA RESOURCES

Visit **abdokids.com** to access crafts, games, videos, and more!

Use Abdo Kids code

CCK7205

or scan this QR code!